BY SUZANNE SELFORS

Wedgie & Gizmo

Wedgie & Gizmo vs. the Toof

SUZANNE SELFORS

WEDGIE & GIZMO

VS. THE TOOF

Illustrated by

Barbara Fisinger

KATHERINE TEGEN BOOKS
An Imprint of HarperCollinsPublishers

This book is for Skylos, my muse.

FAMILY

Mom

Jasmine

Jackson

Wedgie

ALBUM

Abuela

Dad

Gizmo

Elliot

CHAPTER 1

Gizmo

GREETINGS, DEAR READER.

Most of you already know who I am. But in case you are new to this planet, or you have spent the last year frozen in a block of ice and are not up-to-date on important matters, I shall introduce myself.

My name is Gizmo, and I am an Evil Genius.

According to Elliot's comic book collection, which I enjoy reading, all Evil Geniuses have the same goal as I have. . . .

TO TAKE OVER THE WORLD!

Thus far, no Evil Genius has been successful in taking over the entire world. But I will change that. It is my promise to you that I will be the very first Evil Genius who will rule from sea to sea, mountain to mountain, pet store to pet store. Prepare yourself for the day when King Gizmo is seated on his Evil Throne!

I should note that I am different from other Evil Geniuses because I am a cavy. For reasons I do not understand, humans tend to call my kind *guinea pigs*. How insulting! Pigs are lowly creatures who muck about in the mud. Cavies are noble creatures who nap in the sun. Pigs eat slop out of buckets. Cavies eat organically grown greens from a plate.

Pigs snort.

Cavies purr.

Speaking of cavies, in order to take over the world, I will need a horde of them to follow me and do my Evil Bidding. And so that brings me to today's Evil Goal: RECRUIT MY CAVY HORDE.

I tried to contact other cavies through my Evil Genius Facebook page, but I have not yet received any messages. I fear that most of my kind live in cages and do not have access to the internet. So I realize that I need a more primitive way to reach them. Thus, I designed a flyer.

I WANT YOU

FOR MY CAVY HORDE.

Are you tired of living in a cage?
Would you like to meet other cavies?
Waddle through foreign lands?
Eat whatever you like?

Then join my horde today and help me
TAKE OVER THE WORLD!
Signed, Gizmo the Evil Genius

But how can I deliver this flyer and make sure it gets into the paws of cavies everywhere? I scratch my furry chin and ponder.

DAD: Hi, Elliot. Hi, Jasmine. How was school?

ELLIOT: It was okay.

JASMINE: Elliot got a trophy for shooting the most baskets in a contest.

DAD: Really?

ELLIOT: It's no big deal. I've got lots of trophies.

JASMINE: I've never gotten a trophy. Not for anything.

Why must those humans always speak so loudly and disturb my important Evil Thoughts? What a nuisance they are. The only one of whom I am fond is Elliot. He is my servant. He provides me with fresh snacks, changes my litter, and delivers sticks for chewing. We cavies like to chew. It keeps our teeth sharp and perfectly proportioned. An Evil Genius must always look his best.

MOM: Elliot! Jasmine! Come get a snack!
ELLIOT: Great, 'cause I'm starving!

Elliot picks me up. I grunt with annoyance. Where are we going? I am very busy using my Evil Brain. But then I squeak with glee as we enter one of my favorite rooms in this new house. It is the place where the humans store their edibles.

I sniff the air. So many delightful scents fill my quivering nostrils. My tummy rumbles as Elliot sets me onto the counter. Will he give me an apple slice? Or a strawberry top? Or perhaps he will give me the treasure of all human foods—a marshmallow! These humans never feed me marshmallows. I have heard them say they are bad for me and will make me sick. Such nonsense.

They simply do not wish to share!

But wait. What is that commotion? The girl child has entered the kitchen. I grunt at her, but she does not heed my warning. She scoops me up, squeezes me, then plants kisses on my forehead. I understand why she wants to kiss me. I am quite handsome, with soft, velvety fur, and I am perfectly plump all over. She cannot resist me. Who could?

But being squeezed is most unpleasant! I bite her finger. She releases me. It is a trick I have taught her. Now, if only I can teach her to give me a marshmallow.

What's this? My ears perk. My heart skips a beat. Alas, I hear the familiar sound of nails clicking against the floor. I peer over the edge of the counter and glare at what I see. It is the canine who lives in this house. The *dog*. He looks up at me. He wags his tail, even though it's not a long tail, just a stub. He smiles sweetly, but he is not fooling me.

The humans call him Wedgie, but I know him by his true name. He is a corgi, and when he wears the red cape of Thor, he becomes . . .

THORGI, my archenemy!

CHAPTER 2

Wedgie

MY NAME'S WEDGIE, AND I'M A VERY HAPPY dog because it's snack time. I LOVE snack time! I stand in the kitchen next to Jasmine and Elliot and Jackson. They're my pack. I LOVE my pack! My most important job is to protect my pack. That's why I always wear my cape. When I wear my cape, I'm Super Wedgie, and I protect my pack with my superpowers.

Like the power of digging.

And the power of chasing.

And the power of herding.

But right now I want a snack. I'm wagging my stubby tail. Snacks make me so happy. I like all food. I like dog food, and cat food, and fish food. But people food is the very best. I smell cookies. I wag extra hard.

Hey, I'm down here. Can I have a snack?

Something is squeaking. I look up. Furry Potato's on the counter. Hello, Furry Potato! I LOVE the Furry Potato! I like to smell him all over, but I can't reach him. I jump. And jump. And jump. But he's way up there, and I'm way down here.

JASMINE: Mom, they handed this out at school today.

CLOVERLAND ELEMENTARY'S
Parade of Pets

6 pm–7 pm, Tuesday, September 23,

in the Gymnasium

All pets must be in carriers or on leashes.

All dogs must be friendly.

Trophies awarded for: Best Trick, Prettiest Pet,

and Best Owner/Pet Look-alike

JASMINE: Can I take Wedgie again this year?

MOM: Last year he got into a lot of trouble, remember? He chased that cat, and he ate the principal's speech.

JACKSON: And he pee-peed on the floor.

MOM: The principal was very upset.

JASMINE: I know, but he'll be better this year. I won't let him off the leash. I promise.

MOM: Okay, as long as he behaves himself.

JASMINE: Yay! Did you hear that, Wedgie? We're going to be in the pet parade.

Jasmine's talking to me. She pats my head. She scratches my rump. I lick her face. But she doesn't give me a cookie. Elliot's eating a cookie. Jackson's eating a cookie. Even Dad's eating a cookie. How come no one gives me a cookie? I decide to use my superpower of staring. I sit next to Jackson and stare at him, real hard. I sit very still.

And stare.

And stare.

And stare and stare and stare and stare and stare.

I want that cookie. Please oh please oh please give me that cookie!

My superpower works! Jackson drops the cookie. I open my mouth and catch it before it hits the floor. I eat it superfast so no one

can take it from me. That was a really good cookie. I want another one.

Please oh please oh please can I have another cookie?

> **JASMINE:** The whole school thinks Wedgie's a bad dog, just because he made a mess last year at the parade. If we win, then everyone will know he's the best dog ever! And I'll get a trophy. I mean, we will get a trophy.
>
> **ELLIOT:** Why do you care so much about a trophy? They're no big deal. They give them out for everything these days.

What's that sound? I bark at the sound. I follow the sound onto the porch. A truck is stopping across the street. Some people get out. I bark at the people.

Hey, I'm Super Wedgie, and I just ate a

really good cookie! The people wave. A girl waves. She's holding something.

What's that smell? It's a new smell. It's a bit mushroomy and a bit squirrely. But I've never smelled it before. I want to know what it is because I LOVE this new smell! I run down the walkway. I squeeze under the gate and run across the road.

JASMINE: Wedgie! Bad dog! Come back!

I need to find this new smell. I sniff my way right up to the girl.
She sets something on
the ground.

I stop wagging. I stop panting. I stare real hard. The new smell stares back at me.

I don't know what I'm looking at, but I'm pretty sure I LOVE it!

CHAPTER **3**

Gizmo

AFTER SERVING ME AN APPLE SLICE, ELLIOT carries me back to my Eco Habitat. My Evil Brain buzzes with ideas.

In one of Elliot's comic books, Darth Vader, an Evil Villain, forms an army of Stormtroopers to do his Evil Bidding. I, too, will have my own army, only they will be smaller and furrier, but equally fierce! I must begin my plans to form my Cavy Horde.

First, however, I shall take a post-snack

nap. But why is Thorgi barking outside? Such rudeness. My naps are of the utmost importance. If I do not get enough sleep, I become rather cranky.

And when I get cranky, I bite!

I waddle across the bookcase and hop onto the windowsill. The window is open so I squeeze beneath the crack. The barking is coming from across the street. Why must Thorgi always make such a fuss?

Be quiet! I squeak, shaking a paw at him. After a few more barks, he disappears behind a large automobile that has the words *Moving Van* on the side. It is peaceful again. Thorgi is wise to obey me.

I sit and look at the view. It is quite different from the place where Elliot, his father, and I used to live. There is no snow. No forest. The yard is ringed with palm trees. I lift my face to the sky and let the sun warm my furry cheeks. That is when I notice the bird.

It flies in a circle, then lands on a nearby branch. It is a large bird, black in color. How lucky birds are, to be able to fly wherever they want. A shiver of excitement darts up my furry back. I know what I will do. I will command this bird to carry me to villages and pet stores near and far, so that I can deliver my flyers to cavies everywhere. What a Genius Idea!

I stand on my hind legs and wave at the black bird.

Hello, bird! I call. *I need you to carry me on an important mission.* But the bird ignores me. *Bird!* I squeak. *Pay attention! I have a job for you!* The bird turns and looks at me, but he does not move.

Obey me now or you will feel my wrath! I warn him.

But the bird flies away. It is just as I suspected. He does not understand me because birds have brains the size of a pea. My brain, however, is the size of THREE peas.

I shall have to find another means of travel.

Just as I am about to concoct another Genius Idea, Elliot reaches out the window and grabs me. Then he sets me on his bed. At first I am annoyed by the interruption, but when I see the pile of comic books I smile with glee. Oh joy, it is reading time!

ELLIOT: Look, Gizmo, I got a new Batman comic.

Reading is one of my favorite activities, along with marshmallow eating and nap taking. Whilst Elliot opens his comic, I shuffle through the pile, pushing aside the ones I have already read. Perhaps I will find a story about an Evil Horde.

And that is when I find something unexpected—a catalogue called *Gadgets and Gizmos*. I am quite fond of gadgets. I often use them in my Evil Doings. And the word *gizmo* is one of my favorite words, of course. This catalogue looks like something an Evil Genius should read. I turn the pages until I spy an item that makes my little heart skip a beat.

DREAMING OF DRONES?
WANT TO OWN ONE?

Here's your chance!

Large enough to carry most cameras, but small enough to go unnoticed.

Take aerial photos! Spy on your neighbors!

Good fun!

Large enough to hold a camera? That means it could hold me. Oh happy day! With a bit of clever engineering, I could turn the drone into my own personal flying machine. Darth Vader has his Death Star, and I will have my Drone of Destiny!

I hop up and down with excitement. Imagine what I could do with my own flying machine. How much easier it will be to take over the world if I am not trapped in this human house. The first place I would visit would be Swampy's Pet Shop. How wonderful it would be to see Gweneviere, the love of my life. I have not seen her since Elliot took me from that shop. But I think about Gweneviere every day, and I intend to make her my queen. Won't she be surprised when I swoop from the sky? Gizmo the Evil Genius and Gweneviere, reunited at last!

MOM: How come Gizmo's hopping up and down?

ELLIOT: He does that when he's happy. I think he likes his new home.

MOM: Aw, that's sweet.

DAD: Are you going to take Gizmo to the pet parade?

ELLIOT: No. It sounds kinda dumb.

MOM: It's not dumb. It's fun. There were lots of guinea pigs last year. I bet Gizmo could win Prettiest Pet.

ELLIOT: Gizmo would hate all that attention. He's shy. Besides, I don't need another trophy.

I do not bother to listen to the humans, for I am squeaking with delight. A flying machine will allow me to travel beyond these human walls and locate a large group of cavies. Then I will recruit them.

But where shall I find them? Surely there are more cavies in this town. How exciting! My Evil Plan is about to come true!

Soon, Gizmo the Evil Genius will rule the world!

Muh-ha-ha!

CHAPTER 4

Wedgie

I'M SO HAPPY TO SMELL SOMETHING NEW!
I'm going to sniff it all over, from head to
tail. Hello, little buddy. You have four little
legs. You have two little ears. And you have
a little curly tail. What a funny little tail.
But you don't have much fur, so you aren't a
furry potato. What are you?

JASMINE: Hi. Sorry about my dog. He's not
supposed to run out of the yard.

EMILY: That's okay. Pinkie seems to like him.

JASMINE: Does Pinkie belong to you?

EMILY: Yeah. She's a piglet.

JASMINE: She's soooo cute! And I love her sparkly crown.

Oh look, you have a big wet nose, just like me. You must be a dog! But you're a funny dog. With a funny hat. Hello, Funny Dog. I'm Wedgie, but today I'm Super Wedgie because I'm wearing my cape. Do you have a cape? You sure smell good. I live across the street. Are you going to live in this house? Are you going to be my friend? Look at what I'm doing. When I run around you, I protect you with my superpowers.

EMILY: What's Wedgie doing?

JASMINE: He's trying to herd your pig.
Wedgie's a corgi. Corgis like to
herd things.

EMILY: Pinkie doesn't mind. Look,
she's following him. She must
like him.

JASMINE: Yay! They're friends already!

Jasmine's getting my leash. That means she wants me to take her for a walk. The new girl's getting a leash and putting it on Funny Dog.

Come with me, Funny Dog! I'll show you around. Stay close to me and I'll keep you safe.

This is the

street. They'll call you BAD DOG if you run across the street. And they'll call you VERY BAD DOG if you take a nap in the street. So don't do that. Stay away from the street.

Guess what, Funny Dog? I'm real important around here. Everyone knows me. Everybody's my friend.

NEIGHBOR: Hey, Wedgie, get out of my garden!

OTHER NEIGHBOR: Hey, Wedgie, stop chewing on my newspaper!

ANOTHER NEIGHBOR: Hey, Wedgie, don't poop there!

These are the mailboxes. I like to piddle here. Lots of dogs like to piddle here. Can you smell them? Hey! Brutus piddled here. Brutus lives on the other side of the fence. He always gets into my yard and takes my sticks. I'm gonna piddle where Brutus piddled.

This is Duck Pond. They'll call you BAD DOG if you chase the ducks.

And this is my yard. And this is my house. Come on, Funny Dog, let's go inside.

Jackson's running toward us. He's got two cookies in his hands. He gives one to me and one to Funny Dog. We eat our cookies. Then we sniff each other again. I LOVE Funny Dog! And she LOVES me! We're friends. This is the best day ever!

We're going into Elliot's room. That

means Funny Dog will meet Furry Potato. I'm so happy about that! I bark real loud, to let Furry Potato know that I have something important to show him.

Furry Potato is gonna LOVE Funny Dog!

CHAPTER 5

Gizmo

WHAT A GENIUS I AM, TO HAVE FOUND THE drone in the *Gadgets and Gizmo*s catalogue. At the bottom of the page, there is an order form. I begin to chew around the edges of this form. I will fill it out, then mail it. The day my Drone of Destiny arrives will be written about in history books as one of the most important days ever!

But just when the order form is in my little paws, my ears prick. Someone is approaching. I hear panting. Then paw steps. Followed by smaller paw steps. Elliot's bedroom door bursts open.

Oh drat! The girl named Jasmine and the dreaded Thorgi barge in. Double drat! They are followed by another girl and a small dog. I grunt with displeasure. One canine is bad enough, but two are most unpleasant. I plug my nose. Why must canines smell so horrid? Do they not understand the importance of bathing?

JASMINE: Elliot, we've got new neighbors. This is Emily. She's moving into the red house today. Emily, this is Elliot. Our parents just got married so he's my new brother.

ELLIOT: Hi.

EMILY: Hi.

JASMINE: Emily's going to our school. She's in my grade.

ELLIOT: Cool.

This human conversation does not interest me. I begin to make my escape, but Jasmine reaches down and lifts me off Elliot's bed. The order form falls from my paws. As it lands on the carpet, Thorgi grabs it. I squirm.

Stop him! I squeak. But Thorgi tears the order form to shreds. Then he smiles at me. Oh foul beast! How dare you try to stop my Evil Plans!

JASMINE: Emily, this is Elliot's guinea pig,
Gizmo.

EMILY: He sure squeaks a lot. Why does
he wear glasses?

ELLIOT: He's nearsighted. If he doesn't
wear them, he bumps into things.

JASMINE: Elliot, this is Emily's pig, Pinkie.

ELLIOT: How come Pinkie's wearing
a crown?

EMILY: Because she's a princess.

What is this I hear? A princess? Is there
royalty in the room? Well, it is about time
the humans introduced me to someone worthy of my attention. After all, I am destined
to be King Gizmo. Therefore, I should make
other royal friends. Let me meet this princess.

Suddenly, I find myself staring at a face,
the likes of which I have never before seen.
What is this creature? The skin is pink with
little wiry hairs. The eyes are black and

beady. And the nose, why, it is not a nose at all. It is a snout, with enormous nostrils. The creature sniffs me. And grunts. I shudder.

Oh horror of horrors! I know what this creature is. She is a pig! The very same creature for which the humans have named me.

Then I notice a terrible tooth jutting up from her lower lip. I am an admirer of teeth, but this particular tooth is crooked and much too large for her face. This creature needs to see a dentist immediately.

JACKSON: Your pig has a funny toof.

EMILY: Toof? That's so adorable.

JACKSON: I'm gonna call her Pinkie the Toof.

ELLIOT: She and Wedgie seem to like each other.

EMILY: They're instant friends, just like me and Jasmine.

JASMINE: Yeah. Instant friends.

A crown is perched on the pig's pink head. I was not aware that pigs have royal bloodlines. Even so, it does not change the fact that she is still a *pig*. When I host royal parties, I will not be inviting creatures who wallow in mud. I bite Jasmine's finger so she will let go of me.

JASMINE: Ow!

Jasmine sets me into my Eco Habitat. I stick my head out the window and peer down at Thorgi. He thinks that just because he wears a superhero cape, he has the power to destroy me. What a fool he is!

I smile to myself, for what Thorgi does not know is that I do not need the order form to get my Drone of Destiny. At the first opportunity, I will use the computer and place my order online.

Muh-ha-ha!

I crawl back into my sleeping chamber and curl up for my pre-supper nap. I am so very fatigued. The work of an Evil Genius is endless.

CHAPTER 6

Wedgie

IT'S ALMOST TIME FOR THE BUS. THE BUS brings Jasmine home. I LOVE Jasmine! It also brings Elliot home. I LOVE Elliot! It's almost time. I wag my stubby tail. I wag some more. I can hardly wait. The bus makes me so happy!

There it is! I hear the engine at the end of the street. I hear the wheels rolling.

Hey, people! The bus is coming! I run in circles in front of the door. Round and round and round. My cape flaps. I'm using my superpowers to open the door.

MOM: Wedgie, calm down!

JACKSON: Wedgie, do you wanna go out?

I bark and bark because I'm so happy. The door opens. My superpowers worked! I dart outside. Let's go meet the bus!

I dash down the walkway and wait by the gate. The bus is coming. There it is. I see it. It's right down there. Do you see it, Jackson? Do you see it, Mom? The bus is coming. Here it comes. Closer. And closer. It's almost here. I can see the driver. I can see the kids. Here it comes.

The bus is here!

The bus stops and the door opens. Jasmine and Elliot get off. So does Emily, the new girl. They all pet me. They scratch my head, my back, and my rump. I sniff everyone's ankles. Elliot's ankles smell like the bus.

Jasmine's ankles smell like socks. Emily's ankles also smell like socks and like Funny Dog. Where's Funny Dog? Can I play with Funny Dog?

Emily waves good-bye and crosses the street to her house. I bark good-bye, then I herd Jackson, Jasmine, Mom, and Elliot into our house. It's snack time. I LOVE snacks! And today the snacks are muffins. Muffins are soft, and they make crumbs on the floor. I LOVE crumbs! I start licking them up.

Jackson's got a muffin. It's right there. Right in front of my face. Just sitting in his hand. It looks so good. I start drooling. That muffin's the yummiest thing I've ever seen.

I gotta eat it. I gotta eat it right now! I stand on my hind legs. Then I snatch it from Jackson's hand.

JACKSON: Wahhhh!

MOM: Wedgie! Bad dog!

JASMINE: Jackson, you can't put your food so close to the ground or Wedgie will get it.

JACKSON: But *I'm* close to the ground 'cause I'm little.

ELLIOT: He's got a point.

Mom tries to catch me, so I crawl under the couch. Oh muffin, you're so tasty. You're so crumbly. I LOVE you, muffin. But Mom calls me Bad Dog again. I can see her feet. She's waiting for me to come out. But there are more crumbs to eat so I stay under the couch. I stay under the couch for a long time because I know I'm in trouble. Hiding is one of my superpowers. Oh look, Furry Potato

left a little poop under the couch. I eat it. I
LOVE Furry Potato poop!

MOM: Here's another muffin, Jackson.

JASMINE: Can I save a muffin for Emily?
I'm so glad she moved here. We
like the same food and the same
music. She's my new best friend.

MOM: That's nice.

JASMINE: Oh look, Emily's outside. And she
brought Pinkie!

MOM: Why don't you go out and play
with her?

The room gets very quiet. I crawl out from under the couch. I sniff the air. Where's Jasmine? Where are Elliot and Jackson? I sneak past Mom, then run outside.

I found them! Emily and Funny Dog are here too! Hello, Funny Dog. I'm so happy to see you. I sniff her all over. She sure has a funny little tail. But wait. Everyone's petting Funny Dog but no one's petting me. I push against Jasmine. I squeeze between Elliot's feet. I bark at Jackson. How come Funny Dog is getting all the pets? I feel bad. I whine. Pet me. Please oh please oh please pet me.

JASMINE: Are you going to take Pinkie to the pet parade?

EMILY: Definitely. It'll be fun.

JASMINE: I'm gonna take Wedgie. He got into trouble last year, so it's really important that he wins a trophy this year. I don't want people thinking he's a bad dog.

EMILY: Can Wedgie do any tricks?

JASMINE: Uh . . . not really.

EMILY: Pinkie knows lots of tricks. Sit, Pinkie. Shake, Pinkie. Roll over, Pinkie.

Hey, why's Funny Dog rolling around? And why's everyone still petting her? I don't like it when Funny Dog gets all the pets and scratches. Maybe Funny Dog should go back to her house so I can get all the pets and scratches. But wait! What's that on the ground? It's a dried-up, stinky old slug. I LOVE stinky!

ELLIOT: How's Wedgie gonna win a trophy if he doesn't know any tricks?

EMILY: Look, Wedgie knows a trick. He can roll over.

JASMINE: He's not rolling over. He's rolling on something. Gross!

I rub my back all over the stinky old slug. I feel happy again. Now I have the super-power of STINKY!

Hey, people! I'm stinkier than Funny Dog. Pet me!

CHAPTER 7

Gizmo

DEAR READER,

I am pleased to report that evening has fallen. Cavies are not nocturnal by nature, but I love the late hours. I am currently in the television-watching room with Elliot and the Elderly One. Thorgi is lying on the carpet, disturbing us with his snoring. Elliot has placed fresh greens on a plate for me. I nibble and watch a show called *Wheel of Fortune*. It is an interesting show. If the humans solve

the puzzle, they are rewarded with treasures.
They should invite me to be a contestant. The
ratings would go through the roof!

The current puzzle is:

How easy, yet the humans on the show are confused. They lack my Genius Brain.

Buy an E! I squeak. The Elderly One pats my head.

ABUELA: Smart cavy.

The Elderly One comes from Peru, the country of the Andes Mountains, where cavies roam free. It is also the place where humans eat cavies. I used to worry that the Elderly One would put me into her stew pot. But I have learned that she is a vegetarian, like me. When I rule the world, it will be against the law to eat cavies. Anyone who tries to eat a cavy will feel my wrath!

I munch on a sprig of parsley and glance over my shoulder. I need to use the computer to order my Drone of Destiny. But at the moment, the computer is being used by Jasmine. She is watching canine videos. One canine rolls himself up in a blanket.

Another rides a scooter. Another pushes a shopping cart. Those simpleminded beasts seem happy doing tricks for humans. Never will I do such things. Gizmo the Evil Genius does tricks for no one!

JASMINE: Look, Elliot, this dog's dancing. What a great trick. Do you think I should teach Wedgie to dance?

ELLIOT: I think you should teach him to fly. You know, because he's got that superhero cape. Ha-ha.

JASMINE: I'm serious. He needs to learn something amazing to win Best Trick at the pet parade. Can you help me?

ELLIOT: I've got other stuff to do. Besides, I don't care about the pet parade.

JASMINE: But I need your help. You're supposed to be my brother! Come on, Wedgie. Let's go to my room and practice.

What's this? Thorgi stops snoring and jumps to his paws. He follows Jasmine out of the room. What perfect timing. The computer is mine! I jump off the couch, waddle across the carpet, then I . . .

jump onto a chair . . .

jump onto a table . . .

scurry across the table . . .

leap onto a stool . . .

then jump onto the computer desk.

I sit before the vast screen. Unfortunately, typing is not easy for cavies. The keyboard is not made to fit our little paws. I stretch my arms toward the G and type *Gadgets and Gizmos*. I have to be careful that my tummy does not hit the space bar. I mastered the art of typing long ago when I lived at Swampy's Pet Shop. At night, after the shop closed, I would sit at Mrs. Swampy's desk and write letters to the editor of the local newspaper.

Dear Editor,

I read your article titled "German Shepherd Helps the Police," and I do not approve.

Why should we waste our time reading about canines? They are drooling beasts of lowly intelligence. I demand that you stop writing about them.

Sincerely,
Gizmo the Evil Genius

Dear Editor,

Why are there no stories in your newspaper about cavies? I think your readers would like to read about cavies, for we are the most interesting animals in the world. I demand that you include more cavy news in future editions.

Sincerely,
Gizmo the Evil Genius

Dear Editor,

Once again, there is no cavy news in your paper. Therefore, in protest, I will not read any more issues, but I will continue to use your newspaper to line my cage and collect my droppings, for that is all it is good for.

Sincerely,
Gizmo the Evil Genius

Dear Editor,
YOU SHALL FEEL MY WRATH!

Sincerely,
Gizmo the Evil Genius

After a bit more typing, the drone appears on the screen. How lovely it is. Once again, I imagine myself soaring across the sky, delivering my flyers for all cavies to read.

> **MOM:** Why is Gizmo tapping on the keyboard?
>
> **ABUELA:** He's ordering something.
>
> **DAD:** Ha-ha. Guinea pigs can't type. You have a very good sense of humor, Abuela.
>
> **MOM:** Elliot, please get your pet off the keyboard. He might go to the bathroom on it.
>
> **DAD:** And I think you should go check on your sister. You might have hurt her feelings.
>
> **ELLIOT:** I don't understand why winning at the pet parade is so important to her. It's just a dumb contest.

I am about to click Buy This Item when Elliot picks me up. I wiggle. I squirm. *Put me down!* I command. But he continues to carry me away from the computer. Oh what a dreadful turn of events! He is carrying me into Jasmine's room. I cringe. She will cover me in kisses!

ELLIOT: Hi, Jasmine. How's it going with
Wedgie?

JASMINE: I'm trying to teach him to dance,
but he's not doing anything.

ELLIOT: Maybe try something easier?

JASMINE: But easy won't win. Come on,
Wedgie, dance! We only have six
days to learn!

What is happening in here? The girl is shouting commands at the canine. The canine is ignoring her and chewing on a sock. When I rule the world, no canine would dare ignore me. All dogs will serve me! Should I need holes, they will dig them. Should I need to travel across snow, they will pull my sled. And should my human servants need exercise, the dogs will take them for walks. Oh what a glorious time that will be!

I peer over Elliot's fingers and glare at Thorgi. He is tearing the sock to shreds. Then he looks up and smiles at me. I narrow my eyes. He knows that my computer time was interrupted. This was part of his plan. He wants to stop me from ordering my Drone of Destiny.

You will not stop me! I squeak.

Thorgi is my archenemy, and he must go, once and for all!

I shall get rid of him first thing tomorrow, after my mid-morning nap.

CHAPTER 8

Wedgie

HEY, I JUST HEARD ONE OF MY FAVORITE words.

Beach.

I'm so happy. I LOVE going to the beach!

Dad lifts me into the car. I sit on Jasmine's lap. I stick my head out the window. The wind blows on my face. We pass the grocery store. We pass the post office. We pass the park. But we don't stop at those places because we're going to the beach!

JASMINE: Wedgie, get off my lap. I'm mad at you.

DAD: Why are you mad at Wedgie?

JASMINE: He won't learn a trick.

JACKSON: Ew, Wedgie stinks.

MOM: He's been rolling in something.

ELLIOT: Yuck. Why does he do that?

MOM: Dogs roll in things because they like to stink. In the wild, they cover their own scent to protect themselves.

ELLIOT: Yeah, but Wedgie doesn't live in the wild. He lives in a cul-de-sac.

Why's Jasmine sad? Why doesn't she pet me? She didn't call me BAD DOG. But she pushed me away. What's the matter? How come she doesn't pet me?

We're at the beach! Dad opens the door. I jump out before he can stop me. I run in circles. Round and round. Let's go, people! Let's go to the beach.

Hey! Emily and Funny Dog are here. Wow! What a great day. Emily's wearing her water suit. And Funny Dog's wearing her funny hat. I smell Funny Dog all over. I really LOVE her!

WELCOME TO DOG BEACH.
FRIENDLY DOGS MAY RUN FREE.
PLEASE SCOOP POOP.
HAVE FUN!

I run around Funny Dog. I don't need my leash at the beach. Come on! Let's go play in the sand.

There are dogs everywhere. There's a fluffy dog. There's a spotted dog. There's a black-and-white dog. We chase a ball. We chase a crab. We get our paws wet. We dig in the sand. Funny Dog buries her funny hat in the sand. How fun! I LOVE to bury things! But why is she tugging on my cape with her big tooth? She tugs and tugs. Does she want to play? Funny Dog is my best friend.

I find a stinky clam, and I roll on it.

Now we're going to the Snack Shack. Elliot gets ice cream. Jasmine and Emily get ice cream. Jackson gets ice cream, so I sit close to him. I watch the ice cream drip down Jackson's arm. I lick his arm. It tastes great!

If I use my superpower of staring, Jackson will drop his ice-cream cone. I stare and stare and stare. I stare some more.

I wait. I wag. I want that ice cream so bad! I stare and—

He drops it!

I eat the cone as fast as I can. It's crunchy from the sand. I LOVE crunchy.

Hey, why is everyone watching Funny Dog?

JACKSON: Look, Pinkie the Toof can dance!

EMILY: It's a new trick I taught her last
night. Isn't she a good dancer?

JASMINE: Uh ... yeah, she sure is.

EMILY: Maybe this will be her trick for the
pet parade.

JASMINE: Yeah ... maybe.

ELLIOT: Looks like Pinkie lost her crown.

EMILY: That's okay. I have a whole box of
crowns back home.

Hey, everyone. Stop looking at Funny Dog
and look at me! I'm here. Here I am. See me.
I'm chasing birds. Look at all those birds.

I've never seen so many birds. They've got little stick legs, and they're running across the sand. They're running in different directions. They don't know which way to go. Silly birds. I'd better help them with my superpowers of herding. I run around and around the birds. Look at me herd! The birds try to escape, but I round them up. Now the birds are all going in the same direction.

> **MAN:** Hey! That dog's kicking sand all over my towel!
> **KID:** That dog's trying to eat those birds!
> **LADY:** Stop that dog!
> **JASMINE:** Wedgie! Come here!

I prance back toward Jasmine. My cape flaps in the breeze. She'll be so proud of me. Super Wedgie to the rescue!

Jasmine puts on my leash and starts pulling me away from the beach. I don't wanna leave the beach. I wanna eat more ice cream and chase more birds. I wanna play with Funny Dog. But Jasmine whispers in my ear.

JASMINE: Emily copied our dancing trick. But we'll show her. We'll learn something better, right, Wedgie?

Jasmine looks into my eyes. She smiles at me. She's happy because I helped those birds with my superpowers. She knows that Super Wedgie will always help. I lick her face. I LOVE Jasmine!

CHAPTER **9**

Gizmo

IF YOU ARE A GENIUS LIKE ME, DEAR READER, then you understand the importance of napping. Concocting all those Genius Ideas is exhausting. But imagine being an *Evil* Genius. That takes double the energy.

Therefore, throughout the day, I must rest my Evil Genius Mind so it can recharge.

My nap schedule is posted on my Eco Habitat's front door.

But just as I curl into a comfy ball, someone enters the room. I open one eye. It is the
girl, Jasmine. Oh drat! She will surely pick
me up and cover me with kisses. It is not
her fault that I am so loveable and kissable.
I watch her warily. She stands in front of
Elliot's trophy shelf.

JASMINE: One, two, three, four, five, six, seven ... thirteen trophies? Wow. That's amazing.

She leaves. I open the other eye. Why did she not kiss me? Why did she not squeeze me? She completely ignored me. How rude!

And why is the canine barking? I am trying to take a nap! I grind my teeth with frustration. He knows I intend to vanquish him, thus he is trying to weaken me with a lack of sleep. I will not stand for this!

I crawl out from my sleeping chamber, kick open the front door to my Eco Habitat, and stomp across the bookshelf. Then I press my little nose to the window and look out onto the yard, from whence the barking arises.

Thorgi is digging a hole. I am not surprised by this primitive behavior. Canines certainly know how to waste time. But I am surprised that the royal pig is helping.

Whilst Thorgi digs with his front paws, the pig digs with her snout and over-sized tooth. The canine's stubby tail wags, as does the pig's curly tail. It appears they have become  friends. Why would anyone want to be a friend to a dog or to a pig? How perplexing. And why is that hole so large? It is much too big for a bone or a sock—the usual items the canine buries.

Oh you cursed creatures! I know what you are planning. You are digging a hole large enough for a drone. I rise up on my hind legs, press my front paws to the glass, and holler with all my might. *Thorgi! You will not bury my Drone of Destiny! Do you hear me?*

He and the pig pay me no mind. They continue to dig.

Wait an Evil Minute. If Thorgi and the royal pig are working together, that can only mean one thing—the pig has become Thorgi's sidekick. Of course! All superheroes have a sidekick. Thorgi and the Toof are in cahoots!

I rub my furry chin. So this is my arch-enemy's plan. He got himself a sidekick. He believes that two against one will give him a better chance to defeat me. Like Batman and Robin. Or like Han Solo and Chewbacca. He is mistaken!

I shall vanquish them both!

I am about to concoct a new Evil Plan when two human hands reach down and scoop me up. They are wrinkled, spotted hands. I look into the watery eyes of the

Elderly One. She smiles at me, then carries me to the living room, where she settles onto her throne. It is television-watching time. How lovely. The Elderly One presents me with a cheese puff. It is delicious.

New Evil Plan. I will get rid of Thorgi and the Toof later today. Right now, it's time to nourish my Evil Brain.

CHAPTER **10**

Wedgie

I'M SO HAPPY BECAUSE FUNNY DOG IS HERE. She likes to go for walks. She likes to roll on smelly things. But most of all, she likes to dig, just like me. We are digging a hole. We are best friends. I LOVE Funny Dog!

CHAPTER **11**

Gizmo

THE ELDERLY ONE GIVES ME ANOTHER CHEESE puff, then turns on the television. Today's documentary is about pigs. Why would humans dedicate an entire show to *pigs*? How dreadfully boring. Pigs are ordinary creatures with no real purpose on this planet. I grunt with displeasure.

But wait. What is this I hear? The human on the television screen claims that pigs are one of the smartest animals? I almost choke on my cheese puff. *Pigs?* Intelligent? Has a pig ever sent a letter to an editor? Has a pig ever built an Evil Lair? Has a pig ever taken over the world? No! So what if they can find truffles? A true genius would not waste his time looking for fungus!

> **DAD:** Abuela, what are you doing with Gizmo?
> **ABUELA:** We are watching a show. He likes to watch television.
> **DAD:** Gizmo is watching TV?
> **ABUELA:** *Shhh.* The cavy can't hear if you're talking.

Two more cheese puffs are eaten, and I am bored with this pig nonsense. There are important matters to tend to. I must get to the computer and order my Drone of Destiny. Then I must vanquish both Thorgi and the Toof. So much to accomplish!

I hop off the Elderly One's lap and make

my way to the computer desk. I stretch across the keyboard and open the *Gadgets and Gizmos* website. The personal drone is still sitting in my shopping cart.

Do I want to use the shipping address on file? I select Yes.

Do I want to use the credit card on file? How handy. I select Yes.

Do I want extra-special fast delivery? Yes! Then a message appears.

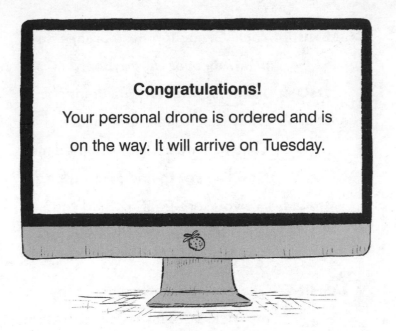

Congratulations!
Your personal drone is ordered and is
on the way. It will arrive on Tuesday.

I clap my paws in glee. Oh what a glorious moment! History has been made today. I wish to celebrate. *Bring me another cheese puff!* I order.

But Jasmine sits at the desk. She does not offer me a cheese puff. She does not squeeze or kiss me. She scoots me aside and begins to type on the keyboard. Once again she ignores me. What could possibly be more important than covering me with kisses?

JASMINE: Yuck, Gizmo left little orange paw prints all over the keyboard.

MOM: Jasmine, what are you doing?

JASMINE: Emily taught her pig to dance. That was my trick. She copied me! Now I've got to find a new trick.

MOM: Are you sure Emily copied you? What if Pinkie already knew how to dance?

JASMINE: Okay, maybe Emily didn't copy my trick, but Pinkie dances better than Wedgie, so I've got to find a new trick. Look at this!

BARKVILLE DOG TRAINING
We've never met a dog
we couldn't train.

I chuckle to myself. Thorgi is going to be *trained*, like an ordinary pet. How humiliating for him. No one trains Gizmo the Evil Genius. If those humans ever tried to train me, they would feel my wrath!

What is this? Elliot is holding a little parsley stem. Oh, I love parsley stems. He spins it clockwise above my head. I spin clockwise. Then he spins it counterclockwise. I spin counterclockwise. Then he presents it to me. I chew with delight.

You see how that works? Elliot thinks he has taught me to spin in a circle. But the truth is, I have taught Elliot to give me the food I want. I have trained him!

Muh-ha-ha!

MOM: Okay, I called Barkville and we can take Wedgie to the trainer this afternoon.

JASMINE: Yay! Elliot, are you gonna come with us?

ELLIOT: I'd rather stay here and read.

MOM: Elliot, this is important to your sister.

ELLIOT: It's not important to me. Why does she care if I'm there?

MOM: Elliot...

ELLIOT: Ugh. Fine.

The humans are wasting their time. Why bother training the canine when I intend to get rid of him? He will soon be gone!

I yawn and stretch my limbs. My Drone of Destiny is ordered and my tummy is full. It is time for my beauty nap. When I awake, refreshed and recharged, I shall begin my second goal of the day—to rid myself of Thorgi and the Toof.

CHAPTER 12

Wedgie

MOM'S GETTING HER KEYS. SHE'S WALKING to the car. Jasmine and Elliot are walking to the car. Are they going for a ride? In the car? I LOVE going for a ride in the car! Hey, can I come too? Can I go for a ride? Please oh please oh please can I go for a ride? I use my superpower of barking.

They call my name. Yes! I'm going for a ride. Are we going to the beach? Are we going to the park?

Where are we going, people?

EMILY: Hi, Jasmine. Hi, Elliot. Where are you going?

JASMINE: Uh . . . nowhere.

ELLIOT: We have to go to a dog trainer because Wedgie doesn't know any tricks.

EMILY: That sounds like fun. Can I come too?

MOM: If your parents say yes, you're very welcome to join us.

EMILY: I'll go ask.

JASMINE: Mom, why'd you invite her? What if she copies Wedgie's new trick?

MOM: I thought you two were best friends.

JASMINE: Yeah, but . . . okay.

Elliot lifts me into the car. I run back and forth across the seat. Where are we going? Oh look, Funny Dog and Emily are getting into the car. Hello, Funny Dog. Do you know where we're going? The car starts moving. I stand on Jasmine's lap and stick my face out the window. The wind smells good. Funny Dog stands on Emily's lap and sticks her face out the other window. Do I like this window? Yes, I do! I walk to the other window. Do I like this other window? Yes, I do! I like both windows. And so does Funny Dog. I LOVE windows! And I LOVE Funny Dog!

The car stops. The door opens, and I jump out. What is this place? I've never been here before. I stick my nose into the air and sniff. I smell dogs. Lots of dogs. I smell the ground, the grass, the rocks. There are dog smells everywhere. This is a dog place. I LOVE dog places!

WELCOME TO
BARKVILLE DOG TRAINING.
WE'VE NEVER MET A DOG
WE COULDN'T TRAIN.

JASMINE: Hi, my name is Jasmine and this is my dog, Wedgie. We made an appointment.

TRAINER: Hi. I'm Molly, the trainer. What a sweet corgi you have. What do you want to teach him?

JASMINE: I want to teach him a trick. Something great.

TRAINER: Oh wow, is that a piglet? That's the cutest thing I've ever seen!

EMILY: She knows lots of tricks.

TRAINER: Really? Like what?

JASMINE: Uh...hello? We're here to teach
Wedgie a trick.

TRAINER: Of course. Well, corgis are usually
really good on the agility course.
Let's give that a try.

We're walking to a big field. There are so
many places to piddle. I LOVE this place!
I meet a shaggy dog. We sniff each other.
We wag.

*My name's Wedgie, but when I wear my
cape I'm Super Wedgie, protector of my pack.*

TRAINER: This is Max. He's a border collie.
Max will show you how the agility
course works. Then Wedgie can
give it a try.

The nice lady takes Shaggy Dog into the
field. Then the lady blows a whistle. Shaggy
Dog starts running. He runs around a stick,
then around another stick. He climbs some

steps. He runs across a log. He climbs down some steps. He jumps over another log. He goes into a tunnel. I whimper. Where is he? But then he comes out the end of the tunnel. Wow! The lady pets him and gives him a treat.

Hey! I want a treat!

The lady talks to Jasmine and hands her a treat. It smells salty and smoky. It smells like the best treat ever. I don't know what it is, but I want to eat it right now. Please oh please oh please give me that treat!

Jasmine walks onto the field. I follow. She blows the whistle. I stare at Jasmine's hand. She points at the stick. I stare at the treat. I jump up and try to get it. She points and blows the whistle. Why does she keep doing that? I drool. I lick my lips. I want that treat. She walks over to the stairs and points. She calls my name. I follow and sit at her feet. I stare at the treat. Oh please give me that treat. Jasmine stomps her foot. She points at the tunnel. I don't care about the tunnel! I want that treat.

How come my superpower of staring isn't working? I scratch her shoe. Don't you love me? I'm a good dog. Please give me that treat.

Hey, what's that? Why, it's Funny Dog. What's she doing? She runs around the sticks. She runs up the stairs. She trots across the log. She runs down the stairs. She leaps over the other log. She goes into the tunnel. I whimper. Where is she? Then she comes out of the tunnel. I'm so happy to see her again! Everyone claps.

Except for Jasmine. Jasmine looks sad. She drops the treat into the grass. I gobble it up!

MOM: Jasmine, what's wrong?

JASMINE: Emily copied me again. She had her pig do the tricks that Wedgie was going to do!

ELLIOT: You think she did it on purpose? I mean, it looked like Pinkie ran the agility course on her own, without Emily's help.

JASMINE: Of course she did it on purpose. She knows how important this is to me. But she wants to win at the pet parade!

The lady is petting Funny Dog. Emily is petting Funny Dog. How come no one is petting me?

I bark. *Pet me! Pet me!* But no one pets me.

JASMINE: Your sign says you've never met
a dog you couldn't train, so how
come it didn't work?

TRAINER: Some dogs take longer. Bring him
back next week and we'll try again.

JASMINE: Next week will be too late. The pet
parade's in four days.

TRAINER: I'm sorry, but we're out of time
today.

EMILY: Did you see Pinkie? She's so smart!
She's the smartest princess pig in
the whole world. I'm going to get a
whole bag of treats for her!

Funny Dog walks over to a fence. I follow
her. *Whatcha doing, Funny Dog?* Funny Dog
shakes her head real hard. Her funny hat falls
off. Then she digs real fast and covers it with
dirt. Are we digging holes? How fun! I want
to dig, too. But Funny Dog starts pulling on

my cape. Why is Funny Dog pulling on my
cape? Hey! This is my cape! Bad Funny Dog!
Bad! I growl. I growl at Funny Dog.

EMILY: Oh no. Wedgie's gonna bite Pinkie!
JASMINE: Wedgie doesn't bite. Pinkie's
being a brat.
EMILY: Pinkie's not a brat!

Jasmine picks me up and puts me in the
back of the car. Why am I back here? I'm
not a Bad Dog. Why am I in the back of the
car? Why is Funny Dog in the front of the
car? Funny Dog sticks her nose out the window. Then she sticks her nose out the other
window. There are no windows back here. I

want a window!

Emily gives Funny Dog another treat. Hey, how come I don't get another treat? Emily gives Funny Dog more pets. How come no one's petting me? Why does Funny Dog get all the treats and all the pets? And why does Funny Dog get all the windows?

I feel sad.

I don't love Funny Dog anymore.

CHAPTER **13**

Gizmo

DEAR READER,

It is early in the morning, and I am sitting in my Eco Habitat, deep in Evil Thoughts. Yesterday I ordered my Drone of Destiny. If it arrives in a timely manner, and if it is in working order, I shall give *Gadgets and Gizmos* a high rating. An Evil Genius appreciates good customer service. Then I will fly away and seek my Cavy Horde. I shiver with anticipation.

Why is the Elderly One staring at me? How rude.

> **ELLIOT:** Hi, Abuela. Is something wrong?
>
> **ABUELA:** Your cavy used my credit card.
>
> **ELLIOT:** Ha-ha-ha. That's so funny.
>
> **ABUELA:** I am not trying to be funny.
>
> **DAD:** Elliot, Abuela, breakfast is ready.

As usual, I ignore the humans and their unimportant conversation. My Evil Task is at hand. Before my Drone of Destiny arrives, I must vanquish Thorgi and the Toof, to keep them from trying to bury it. Having read Elliot's comic books, I am well versed in the tools of superheroes and villains, so I make a list of the ways I can get rid of them.

Ways to Get Rid of Thorgi and the Toof
1. Gamma ray
2. Giant laser beam
3. Kryptonite
4. Shrinking machine

It is a list worthy of my Evil Genius Mind. I sit back and consider these options. A gamma ray would turn Thorgi and the Toof into mutants. But what kind of mutants? Would they be stupider and weaker, slipping in their own puddles of drool? Or would they be gigantic and powerful, with dog and pig breath that could knock a drone from the sky?

I decide against using a gamma ray.

A giant laser beam would sizzle Thorgi and the Toof to a crisp, no doubt about it. But this would leave a rather unpleasant mess, which might be traced back to me. For reasons I cannot fathom, humans are fond of canines and pigs. They actually seem to love them. If the humans know that I sizzled Thorgi and the Toof to a crisp, then the humans might stop serving me. I can't have that!

I cross out *giant laser beam*.

Kryptonite is an interesting option. It was used to foil Superman, the most powerful of all heroes. But it only comes from Planet Krypton. I checked on the computer and apparently that planet does not yet have internet service, so I cannot place an order.

I cross out *Kryptonite*.

Which leaves me with my final option— a shrinking machine. Yes, that does seem to be my best choice, for if I shrank Thorgi and the Toof to the size of fleas, they could not dig a hole to bury my Drone of Destiny. They would be powerless against me. On another note, it is quite possible that they would get sucked into the vacuum machine and we would never see them again.

Oh, what a glorious day that would be!

Shrinking machine it is!

I wonder if *Gadgets and Gizmos* sells a shrinking machine. I bet they do. Now, where did I leave that catalogue? I look around Elliot's room, but it is nowhere to be seen.

> **MOM:** Oh no! Who put my sweater in the dryer?
>
> **DAD:** I did. I was doing a load. Why?
>
> **MOM:** It shrank. The dryer shrank my favorite sweater.
>
> **JACKSON:** Bad dryer!

My little ears prickle. This particular human conversation interests me. I know of this dryer. It is called Maytag. There are many soft fluff balls behind it, which are excellent for nesting. I had already chosen this location for the site of my future Evil Lair. But I did not know that Maytag Dryer was also a Shrinking Machine.

Dear reader, fortune has smiled upon me. I snicker to myself. If I can lead Thorgi and the Toof into the dryer, I can shrink them. Then I will be free to fly my Drone of Destiny to cavies near and far and form my Cavy Horde. Oh happy day!

But how shall I get them into the dryer? It does not take an Evil Genius Mind to figure that out. Canines and pigs think about one thing and one thing only—food. All I have to do is find the food they cannot resist and lure them inside. Soon, they will be the size of gnats. Today is the dawn of a new Evil Day!

Oooh, what have we here? Elliot has brought me a lovely strawberry top. What was I talking about? It was something important, of course. But that strawberry top looks scrumptious. Allow me to pause a moment whilst I enjoy this sweet snack.

CHAPTER **14**

Wedgie

IT'S TIME FOR MY MORNING PATROL, BUT Jasmine's still in bed. Wake up, Jasmine! I walk up the doggy stairs and across the blankets. I find a Cheerio on Jasmine's bed. It tastes great! I lie next to Jasmine. I poke her with my nose. Come on, Jasmine, wake up. The sun's shining. I want to chase squirrels. I want to bark at Brutus. I want to go on patrol. She opens her eyes. I lick her face, but she frowns at me.

JASMINE: Wedgie, why won't you learn a trick?

She sounds sad. Why's Jasmine sad?

Hey, what's that sound? It's outside. I jump and jump and jump, but I can't see. Jasmine picks me up and carries me to the window. I see Emily. And Funny Dog. They're walking. How come Funny Dog gets to go for a walk? I wanna go for a walk. Emily waves. Jasmine opens the window.

EMILY: Hi, Jasmine. Did you see Pinkie's new fancy crown? She got it at the beauty parlor yesterday.

JASMINE: The beauty parlor?

EMILY: Pinkie goes there once a week. That's why she's always so pretty. I bet she could win Prettiest Pet at the pet parade. Hey, do you and Wedgie wanna play?

JASMINE: Oh, no ... we can't. We're super busy. Bye.

Jasmine closes the window. Emily and Funny Dog are walking away. Funny Dog shakes her head. Her funny hat falls off. *Hey!* I bark. *Get your funny hat!* But Funny Dog kicks her funny hat into the bushes. Then she keeps walking away. Jasmine puts me on the floor. Funny Dog gets to go for a walk. Can we go for a walk? Can we? Huh? But then I hear a real important noise.

The refrigerator door's opening!

I run. I run as fast as I can, out of Jasmine's room. I run down the hall. I skid across the floor on my belly. I land right in front of the refrigerator. Look at all that food. Do I see hot dogs? Yes, I see hot dogs. I LOVE hot dogs!

Hey, the refrigerator door is open, but Mom's way over there. Can I get one of those hot dogs? I stand on my back legs and stretch my neck. I stretch and stretch. I got one!

MOM: Wedgie! Bad dog!

Uh-oh. Mom wants my hot dog. But it's mine. I run as fast as I can. I run down the hall. I run into Elliot's room. The hot dog belongs to me! I crawl under Elliot's bed. I'm gonna use my superpower of hiding.

JASMINE: Elliot, can I talk to you?

ELLIOT: I guess.

JASMINE: Wedgie won't learn any tricks so I have to try something else. Do you think he could win Prettiest Pet?

ELLIOT: I don't know. He stinks real bad.

JASMINE: Pinkie went to a beauty parlor, and she looks pretty. And now Emily thinks she'll win Prettiest Pet. Maybe I'll take Wedgie to the same beauty parlor, and he'll be even prettier!

ELLIOT: But wouldn't that be copying? You got mad at Emily for copying you.

JASMINE: Why should I care about Emily's feelings if she doesn't care about mine?

ELLIOT: But isn't your friendship more
important than winning?

JASMINE: Emily copied me first. And maybe
I don't want to be friends with her
anymore. Come on, Wedgie, we're
going to the beauty parlor.

ELLIOT: Can I bring Gizmo, too? He loves
getting a bath.

I hear footsteps. I see Elliot's feet and
Jasmine's feet. I see Mom's feet. Hands
reach under the bed. I scoot backward.

They want the hot dog. But this is my hot dog. I LOVE this hot dog!

I dart across the room. I run down the hall. I am Super Wedgie, and no one can catch me! I run into Abuela's room. I slip under Abuela's bed. I am the best hider!

Oh no, here they come. They reach under the bed. I growl. My hot dog! Mine!

CHAPTER 15

Gizmo

I AM BUSY WITH MY LATEST EVIL PLAN, WHICH I call *Operation: Shrink My Archenemies.* I am sitting on the floor, in front of Maytag Dryer. Spread before me is my drawing of the steps I will take to lure Thorgi and the Toof into the Shrinking Machine. I must be careful that this drawing does not fall into the wrong paws. But I can show you, dear reader. Here it is. Do you see how I called

upon the laws of physics and mathematics?
I am such an amazing artist!

I am about to check the measurements
for Maytag Dryer when Thorgi bounds into
the room. I scowl at him. Why is he here?
My trap is not yet set. Does he suspect my
plans to vanquish him? He has come to spy
on me! He wants to steal my drawing and
show the humans.

I quickly slide the paper underneath Maytag Dryer. Then I prepare myself to be sniffed all over by dog nose. But he does not sniff me. He is more interested in a piece of food, which he begins to devour.

Canines have the worst manners I have ever seen. Do they even chew? I think not. They do not use napkins, either.

But now the girl is here.

JASMINE: Come on, Wedgie. We're gonna make you all pretty so you can win Prettiest Pet. You're gonna have a bath!

As Thorgi is being carried away, a piece of food falls from his mouth. It smells disgusting. How can he eat such things? I would never eat meat. I am a vegetarian of the highest standards. But even though the morsel is revolting, I realize that fate has presented me with a gift. Here is the food that Thorgi cannot resist. Here is my bait.

Operation: Shrink My Archenemies has begun!

I open my Polar Expedition Rucksack and take out a piece of string and a small rock. I tie the string around the rock, then I toss the rock upward. It sails through the handle of

Maytag Dryer and back to me. With both ends of the string in my paws, I pull with all my Evil Strength. Maytag Dryer opens. Step one is complete!

Next, I remove a band from my rucksack. It is an object that Jasmine uses to tie back her hair. I will use it as a sling. I set the piece of meat product into it and pull back. Thanks to my extraordinary aim, the morsel flies right into the dryer.

Too bad there is not an Olympics for cavies. When I become King Gizmo, I will start one. Gweneviere, my future queen, will win the gold medal in wheel waddling. And I shall win the gold medal for everything else. I am pleased with my progress. Step two is complete!

On to step three. I must reach the top of Maytag Dryer, for that is where the Start button lies. This will not be an easy feat. It will take courage and skill. The risk of falling is great, but I refuse to let fear stop me in my quest. How amusing it will be to see Thorgi shrunk to the size of a tick. Won't he be surprised? Muh-ha-ha!

I reach into the rucksack and pull out a rectangular object called chewing gum. I will chew this gum until it becomes sticky, then I will apply it to my paws. The sticky quality will allow me to climb Maytag Dryer in the same way a tree frog climbs a tree.

Then, once I am at the top, I shall wait for Thorgi. He cannot resist food, so he will soon return for his meat morsel.

Once he has jumped into the Shrinking Machine, I will push the Start button.

Then I will repeat the process with the Toof!

As I begin to unwrap the chewing gum, Elliot enters.

ELLIOT: Gizmo, what are you doing in here? I've been looking all over for you.

DAD: Why is there a piece of hot dog in the dryer?

JACKSON: Don't look at me. I didn't do it.

ABUELA: The cavy put it in there.

ELLIOT: How could Gizmo get a hot dog into the dryer? He can't reach that high.

ABUELA: He is a little evil genius.

Before I can start chewing, Elliot lifts me and walks toward the front door. Hold on!

There is nothing on my appointment schedule about taking a journey today. I did not agree to this.

Put me back! I squeak. But alas, we are heading toward the automobile. And now we are inside. The canine is here, too. Why is he whining and shaking?

This interruption could not have come at a worse time. I was so close to achieving my goal. But now *Operation: Shrink My Archenemies* is delayed. I shake my fist and squeak. *Wherever we are going, there had better be a lovely four-course lunch set out for me, or I will get very grumpy and start biting.*

I curl into a ball and close my eyes for my pre-lunch nap.

CHAPTER **16**

Wedgie

BATH!!

CHAPTER 17

Gizmo

WHEN I AWAKE FROM MY PRE-LUNCH NAP, I find that Elliot is still holding me, but we are no longer in the car. We are standing in front of a store.

Pretty Paws
A Beauty Parlor
for Pets

Elliot carries me into the shop. Pardon me? This is an outrage! I do not need to be beautified. I am already a specimen of utter loveliness. My fur is spectacular. My teeth are polished. And my rump is sparkly clean. How can you possibly perfect that which is already perfect?

A horrid whining sound fills the room. The girl tugs on Thorgi's leash.

JASMINE: Come on, Wedgie. It won't be so bad. They're gonna make you beautiful.

I smile smugly. Why, of course. This field trip to the beauty parlor is for the canine, not for me. Finally those humans are going to do something about his appearance. His fur is always a mess and that ragged cape is out of style. Whoever told him that red is his color was seriously mistaken.

Jasmine pulls him inside, then quickly

shuts the door. Thorgi is still whining. What is it, exactly, that frightens him? I must know!

LADY: Welcome to Pretty Paws. How may I help you?

JASMINE: Can you make my dog look pretty? Really pretty? So we can win the Prettiest Pet trophy?

LADY: Of course we can make him pretty. Our doggie dream special includes shampoo, conditioning and detangling, nail trim, nail polish, tooth cleaning, and ear cleaning.

JASMINE: That sounds great.

LADY: And what are we doing with the guinea pig?

ELLIOT: Gizmo and I don't care about the contest. I just brought him because he really loves taking a bath.

LADY: Of course. We have little tubs right over there.

Elliot sets me onto a counter and begins to fill a tub with water. I clap my hands with glee. How wonderful! I do so love baths. Elliot puts a little cap on my head, to protect my ears. Then he sets me into the tub. The water is neither too hot nor too cold. He takes a little scrub brush and washes my tummy. He is such a good servant. I have trained him well.

You might be surprised to learn this, dear reader, but we cavies are excellent swimmers. When I was a pup at Swampy's Pet Shop, I would practice in the goldfish tank. Even the fish were in awe of my backstroke.

Splashing and howling interrupt my peace. I peer over the edge of my tub. Thorgi is in another tub. He is trembling and squirming. What is the matter with him? Now he is running across the store, trying to escape. He leaves trails of water wherever he goes. He darts under a table, overturns a display of leashes, then slides across the floor and careens into a stack of towels. What a mess he is making. Elliot's father carries him back to the tub. Then Jasmine sprays water on him, and he whimpers. Is it true? The great superhero Thorgi is afraid of water? How pitiful.

I am fluffed with a towel. My glasses are cleaned. I lie on a cushion and stretch out my paws. The nice serving lady clips my nails and buffs them. I smile at Elliot. He brought me here because he knows that soon I will be King Gizmo, and he wants me to look my best. When I am king, I shall erect a statue in Elliot's honor.

Thorgi has stopped whining. He is dried and brushed and seems happy to be out of the water.

LADY: As a final touch, we give our clients a tiara or a bandana.

JASMINE: Ooh, I'll take a red bandana. That'll look great on Wedgie.

What have we here? The lady is holding a tiny crown in her hand. For me? Finally! My crown has arrived. I reach out and grab it. Then I plunk it onto my head.

It fits perfectly. I admire my reflection in the mirror. How regal I look. How handsome. King Gizmo has arrived.

CHAPTER 18

Wedgie

IT'S OVER. THE BATH'S OVER. WHY DID THEY do that to me? Why did they put me in the water? That felt bad. Really really bad. I shake off the water. I shake and shake until I'm dry.

Now I feel good. I feel bouncy. I'm so happy. I'll never have to take a bath again!

DAD: Wow, Wedgie looks great.

JASMINE: Do you think he's prettier than Pinkie?

MOM: He's pretty in his own way.

JASMINE: But do you think we have a chance to win Prettiest Pet?

DAD: Of course you have a chance.

JACKSON: Wedgie smells like a flower.

Hey, what's this around my neck? I don't like this new thing. Where's my cape? I

shake and shake until the new thing falls off. Good-bye, new thing.

> **MOM:** You know who might win Prettiest Pet? Gizmo. He looks so glamorous in that tiara.
>
> **JASMINE:** Oh no, you're not going to enter Gizmo in the contest, are you?
>
> **ELLIOT:** I told you guys, I don't care about those contests. Neither does Gizmo.
>
> **JASMINE:** Phew! You hear that, Wedgie? We still have a chance.

We're home again. I'm so happy to be home. I don't like that bad place where they make you take a bath. But I LOVE home. I jump out of the car. Brutus is lying on the other side of the fence.

Hey, Brutus, I bark. *Don't ever go to that bad place where they make you take a bath!* Brutus doesn't say anything, but I know he's happy I warned him. That's what I do. I'm Super Wedgie, and I protect my family and my friends.

I'm about to run into the house when I smell something. I turn in circles, sniffing and sniffing. Oh look, the stinky old slug is still here. I LOVE that stinky old slug. I'm gonna roll all over it so I can be stinky too.

JASMINE: WEDGIE! NOOOOOOOO!!!

CHAPTER 19

Gizmo

TODAY IS TUESDAY, WHICH MEANS . . . DRUM roll, please . . . this is the day I receive my Drone of Destiny. The mail delivery human always arrives sometime between mid-morning nap and post-lunch nap, so I may have to wait awhile. But do not worry. I brought snacks. An Evil Genius *always* has snacks. I squeeze beneath the window and sit on the sill, watching for the brown truck.

The sun is shining. The neighborhood

is quiet. Most of the human children are at school, hoping to become geniuses like me. Even Thorgi is quiet. He lies in the grass, staring through the fence posts. What is he staring at? I stretch to get a better view. A pink snout and two beady black eyes are looking through the fence posts across the street. Thorgi whimpers. Why are Thorgi and the Toof separated? Whatever the reason, this is a welcome turn of events.

> **MOM:** What's wrong with Wedgie?
>
> **JACKSON:** He's sad. He wants to play with Pinkie the Toof.
>
> **MOM:** Oh dear. Well, Jasmine and Emily seem to be in some kind of fight. It's too bad. I hope they figure it out.

As I nibble on a celery stick, I ponder yesterday's events. It is true that *Operation: Shrink My Archenemies* did not come to fruition. It was interrupted by an unexpected trip to the beauty parlor. Whilst I was annoyed by this detour, it turned out that Elliot took me there so he could bestow me with my crown. He wants me to look my best when I introduce myself to my future Cavy Horde. What a loyal servant.

But today I must keep Thorgi and the Toof from intercepting my delivery. Thus, I sit and wait.

The day is most pleasant. The sun is shining. Flowers are blooming. As I nibble, a brown truck stops at the curb. A woman jumps out. She is carrying a package. My heart doubles its rhythm. Can it be?

She opens the gate and walks toward the front porch. I pull my Barbie Binoculars from my Polar Expedition Rucksack and peer through the lenses. I spy a *Gadgets and Gizmos* logo on the box. I hop up and down with excitement. My Drone of Destiny is here! Oh glorious day!

But my excitement is quickly dashed, for Thorgi has jumped to his paws and is barking at the mail delivery person. What dastardly deed is this? He runs around and around the woman's feet, trying to trip her.

Once again I have underestimated Thorgi's cleverness. I thought he was being lazy, but he was lying in wait to intercept my Drone of Destiny and bury it in his hole. Curse you, foul beast!

Shall I fling myself upon him and bite him on the nose? That would teach him a lesson. But from my perch on the windowsill, I am too far away. So I must do something else. The mail delivery person stops walking as Thorgi circles her. She is trapped! I quickly shuffle through my Polar Expedition Rucksack, looking for a means to stop my canine enemy.

Aha! I wrap my paw around a granola bar that I was saving for my air travels. I find another hair band. These should work perfectly.

I make a mental map in my head.

I remove the wrapper, set the granola bar into the band, take aim, pull, and . . . release!

The granola bar soars through the air. I clap my paws. The anticipation is almost too much to bear.

The granola bar sails over the grass . . .

bounces off a tree . . .

and hits the mail delivery person right on the head.

Oops.

Did I miscalculate? That is not possible. My aim is always true and swift. A gust of wind must have interfered. The mail delivery person rubs her head. The bar is stuck in her hair. She reaches up, grabs it, and tosses it aside. Thorgi stops barking. He turns and chases after the snack. My Evil Plan worked after all!

The mail delivery person walks up the front porch and hands the package to Elliot's father. I am breathless with joy.

DAD: Abuela, you have a delivery.

ABUELA: It's not for me. It's for the cavy.

DAD: You bought something for Gizmo?

ABUELA: No, he bought it for himself. He used my credit card.

JACKSON: Bad Gizmo.

DAD: It's a drone! Abuela, why would you order a drone?

ABUELA: I didn't. Why does no one believe me?

MOM: A drone is way too dangerous for the kids. I really think you should send it back.

My Drone of Destiny is here. Now I must pack for my flight. I squeeze back under the windowsill and scurry to my Eco Habitat. Before she moved to the Land of Goodwill, Barbie left a lot of equipment behind, some of which I have placed in my storage chamber.

I sort through the pile and find a pair of pink aviator goggles to protect my eyes from the wind, a pink scarf to keep my furry neck warm, and a water bottle to keep me hydrated. I find a nice array of snacks in my food chamber—sunflower seeds, timothy hay pellets, and some Cheerios.

I feel giddy with excitement. I am about to take flight! I am about to find my Cavy Horde!

But perhaps I should first take a nap. Yes, a nap is exactly what I need. Then I will set forth. An Evil Genius cannot form an Evil Horde without a good long nap.

CHAPTER 20

Wedgie

THE SCHOOL BUS IS HERE. ELLIOT GETS OUT.
He pets me. Jasmine gets out. She pets me.
Everyone is petting me. I turn in circles. I'm
so happy! Emily gets out. Hi, Emily!

> **EMILY:** I'm so excited about the pet
> parade tonight. I've decided to
> enter Pinkie in all of the contests.
> **JASMINE:** All of them? That doesn't seem
> fair.

EMILY: Why not? It'll be more fun that way. Are you going to enter Gizmo in any of the contests?

ELLIOT: Gizmo and I aren't going. Pet contests are dumb.

JASMINE: I don't think they're dumb.

Funny Dog is looking through the fence. I see you, Funny Dog. I see your funny nose and your funny face. Hello. Do you wanna dig a hole? Do you wanna roll on something stinky? Funny Dog sticks her head through the fence. Funny Dog bites my cape. Funny Dog pulls on my cape. Hey! This is my cape. Mine! I growl.

EMILY: Wedgie, don't growl at Pinkie. You're scaring her. You're a bad dog.

JASMINE: He's not a bad dog. Pinkie's the one who's being bad.

EMILY: Pinkie's never bad. She's a princess. I don't think Wedge and Pinkie should play together anymore.

JASMINE: Fine by me!

What's that? Did someone just say BAD DOG? I try to hide behind the mailbox, but Jasmine picks me up. Jasmine carries me up the walkway. Good-bye, Funny Dog! Good-bye, Emily! We're going inside. Are we going to have a snack? That's what we always do. After the bus comes we always have a snack. I lick Jasmine's face. I LOVE snacks!

Now we're inside. Jasmine puts me down. Where are the snacks? I sniff and sniff and sniff.

DAD: Hi, kids. How was your day?

JASMINE: Emily is being really mean. And so is Elliot!

Jasmine is using her angry voice. Why's Jasmine angry? What did I do? I sit. I wonder. I watch Jasmine run down the hall. I whimper. Jasmine?

ELLIOT: How come Jasmine is so grumpy?

DAD: Jasmine used to be the oldest kid and now that you're here, she's the middle kid.

ELLIOT: So?

DAD: Winning one of those trophies is her way of trying to feel special. When you say it's dumb, it hurts her feelings. It would be nice if you supported her.

ELLIOT: Yeah, okay. I get it.

Jasmine's lying on her bed. I'm lying next to her. I LOVE Jasmine's bed. It's soft. I can go under the covers and over the covers. Under the pillows and over the pillows. Sometimes I find a sock. Socks are fun to chew. Shoes are also fun to chew. But today I'm not chewing on anything. I'm cuddling with Jasmine. She's nice and warm.

Jasmine rolls onto her side. I lick her face. Then I cuddle some more. Her hair smells like flowers. I LOVE Jasmine!

Now Elliot's in the room. Hi, Elliot!

ELLIOT: I'm sorry I said the pet parade was dumb. I'll go with you, if you want.

JASMINE: I'm not going! Wedgie won't win Best Trick, and he won't win Prettiest Pet.

ELLIOT: But what about the other contest? Best Look-alike.

JASMINE: Oh, I forgot about that. But it's in two hours. We don't have time to make costumes.

ELLIOT: I have my Thor cape from Halloween. You can have it. And then you and Wedgie will match.

JASMINE: Really? Oh thank you, Elliot!

CHAPTER 21

Gizmo

I AM IN THE MIDST OF A WONDERFUL DREAM.
I am flying my Drone of Destiny, the wind at
my back, fame and fortune ahead. As I pass
over neighborhoods, cavies scurry out of
their human houses. They raise their paws
and catch my flyers. Then they wave and
cheer me onward. As I pass over pet stores,
more cavies appear, collecting my flyers and
waving to me, their future king. It is glorious. The uprising has begun!

But someone grabs me, and I am rudely awakened. What is happening? I did not make any appointments. I need to get my sleep. Set me down immediately!

ELLIOT: Sorry, Gizmo, but we're all going to the pet parade to support Jasmine. You have to come with us if you want to be in the parade.

I stop struggling. A parade? I am going to be in a parade? Well, this is certainly a pleasant turn of events. The humans have finally come to understand my importance, and they are throwing a parade in my honor.

I had planned on taking my first flight this very evening. My Polar Expedition Rucksack is packed and ready to go. But if there's a parade in my honor, I suppose I could delay my departure. I wouldn't want to disappoint my fans. I make little noises of contentment. A Drone of Destiny *and* a

parade. Today is shaping up quite nicely.

When I am King Gizmo, this parade will become an annual tradition. An official holiday. It will be televised so everyone can see me sitting on my throne, high on a float, waving to the crowd. My human servants will toss marshmallows and there will be music and fireworks. I will need a theme song.

Take me to my parade! I command as I grab my crown. *Let us not keep the masses waiting!*

Elliot sets me in a small portable chamber, then carries me to the automobile. The canine paces back and forth. He is jealous. The citizens of this town have chosen to honor me, and it is obviously driving him crazy.

But what do I see? The girl is wearing a cape that matches Thorgi's cape. She has joined his side! I should have expected this. But I am not worried. Thorgi thinks he can thwart me with two sidekicks. He is delusional. When we return home, I shall shrink them all in the Shrinking Machine. I will be victorious because my Evil Brain is the size of THREE peas!

During the car ride, I prepare my speech. I will thank my littermates, who taught me the importance of hiding food and not sharing. I will also thank Swampy's Pet Shop, for that is where I learned to read and write. I will thank Elliot for his loyalty and devotion. And I will thank Gweneviere for agreeing to become my future queen.

Of course, I must also thank myself, for

without me and all my hard work, I could never Take Over the World!

Then I will tell the audience that if they eat a nutritious diet, treat themselves to a tasty marshmallow now and then, and take lots of naps, they, too, can become Evil Geniuses.

But then I shall laugh and tell them I am kidding. No one can be like me!

As I conclude my speech, I will instruct everyone that the autograph line will form to the right, and please no pushing or shoving. Then I will bow as applause fills the air.

What a glorious moment that will be!

The car stops. Elliot keeps me in my portable chamber so that I will not be crushed by the admiring crowd. I set my crown onto my head and fluff up my fur. I make certain that no green bits cling to my teeth. There will be many photographs, and I must look my best.

We stand outside a building called Cloverland Elementary School. A banner hangs above the door.

Welcome to Cloverland Elementary's
PET PARADE

Why is my name not on the banner? Humans are so lazy.

Elliot carries me into the building. It is noisy inside. There is squawking, barking, meowing, and chirping. The humans have brought their pets to meet me. I wave from my portable chamber.

PRINCIPAL: Hello, Elliot. What a nice guinea pig.

ELLIOT: His name is Gizmo.

PRINCIPAL: You can put him on the table with the other small pets.

Hold on a minute. Did that human just call *me* a pet? I am not a pet. I am an Evil Genius, and I am supposed to be placed on a podium or a stage of some sort. So I can give my speech before the parade commences. Where is my microphone? My spotlight?

Elliot walks along a table. I peer through the bars of my portable chamber. We pass a cage containing a white rat. The rat eyes me suspiciously. I admire rats. They are intelligent, and they can carry plague, which is quite Evil indeed. This particular rat might like to become one of my minions. I will discuss the details with him later.

We pass a cage containing a pair of gerbils. They are giggling and hiding in a toilet paper roll. Gerbils are brainless creatures. I have no use for them.

But then we come to a section of the table where all the cages contain cavies. I grasp the bars of my chamber. I have not seen other cavies since leaving Swampy's. What a beautiful sight! Short-haired cavies. Long-haired cavies. Fat cavies. Skinny cavies. Cavies with spots. Cavies without spots. Elliot sets me down, then walks away.

Hello, I say. *I am Gizmo the Evil Genius, and I am your future king.* They pay me no mind because they cannot hear me. A parrot is squawking, *Pretty boy, pretty boy,* and some dogs are barking.

I squeak as loudly as I can. *Join my Cavy Horde and help me take over the world!* But the cavies do not reply. How can I get their attention?

Human children stick their fingers into my portable chamber. How rude! I bite a finger. Where is Elliot? Where is my parade? I fold my arms and scowl.

I will write a letter of complaint to the leader of Cloverland Elementary. It is very rude to make the guest of honor wait!

The door to my container opens. I see a
spotted human hand. It reaches in and pulls
me free. I look into the watery eyes of the
Elderly One.

ABUELA: This came in the mail for you. They want me to return it, but it's yours. This'll teach them to think I'm crazy!

CHAPTER 22

Wedgie

OH BOY, I LOVE THIS PLACE. THERE ARE ANImals everywhere. I see cats. I see rabbits. I see dogs. There's a big dog. There's a dog with a smooshed face. There's a dog with no fur. Hey, what happened to your fur? I'm getting lots of pets. And lots of scratches. I LOVE pets and scratches!

There are so many smells in here. I smell popcorn. I smell cookies. I smell lots and lots of dogs.

Jasmine holds tight to my leash. I wanna go smell the dogs. I tug and tug and tug. But she won't follow me.

PRINCIPAL: You brought Wedgie?

JASMINE: He'll be good this year. I promise.

PRINCIPAL: I certainly hope so. He was such a bad dog last year. He almost ruined everything.

JASMINE: He's not a bad dog. You'll see.

PRINCIPAL: Just make sure you keep him on that leash. And keep him away from the cats. Oh, look at that adorable piglet over there. She looks just like a princess.

Why are they sitting when there are so many things to smell? Dad tells me to sit. Mom tells me to stop barking. I smell Jackson's ankles. They smell like home. I LOVE home. I rest my head on Jackson's foot.

PRINCIPAL: Ladies and gentlemen, welcome to Cloverland Elementary's pet parade. We have three contests tonight, but we won't announce the winners until the very end. Our first contest is for Best Trick.

Big Dog's in the middle of the room. A boy's with him. The boy holds up a hoop. Big Dog jumps through it. Everyone claps. Can I have some popcorn?

Now Dog with Smooshed Face is in the middle of the room. A girl's with him. Dog with Smooshed Face picks up a newspaper and carries it to the girl. Everyone claps. I need to piddle. Can we go outside and piddle?

Hey, Funny Dog's in the middle of the room. I jump to my paws. Hello, Funny Dog! Whatcha doing over there? Funny Dog shakes her head. Her funny hat slides across the floor. Then she runs. Emily chases her.

EMILY: Pinkie, come back. Why won't you sing and dance like we practiced?

PRINCIPAL: Let's give a big round of applause to Emily and Pinkie for trying. Our next contest is for Prettiest Pet.

I really, really, really want some popcorn. It smells so salty. Can I have some popcorn? Why do I have to sit? Why do I have to stay? A long time passes. A really really really long time. I whimper. Why can't I go play with the other dogs?

EMILY: Pinkie, please come out from
under the table. Don't you want
to be Prettiest Pet?
PRINCIPAL: Well folks, let's have a round of
applause for all those super-
pretty pets. Now it's time for the
look-alike contest.

Jasmine tugs on my leash. I don't have
to sit! I don't have to stay! We walk out to
the middle of the room. There's Funny Dog
again. I want to smell her. But Jasmine pulls
me away. Funny Dog and Emily are both
wearing funny hats. Funny Dog shakes her
head. Her funny hat falls off.

EMILY: Pinkie, why won't you wear your
crown? We're both supposed to
be princesses.

Funny Dog kicks her funny hat. Then
she trots up to me. Hi, Funny Dog. Look at

me and Emily. We both have capes. Hey! Why is Funny Dog pulling on my cape? She pulls so hard, it comes off. Now Funny Dog is running away with my cape. Are we playing chase? I LOVE playing chase! I'm gonna get you, Funny Dog!

But what's that sound? I've never heard that sound before. I look up.

Hey! It's the Furry Potato. What's he doing way up there?

CHAPTER **23**

Gizmo

THE ELDERLY ONE BROUGHT **MY** DRONE OF Destiny! This is a delightful turn of events. The Elderly One has become my servant. Not only do we watch television and eat cheese puffs together, but she clearly shares my vision and wants to help me with my Evil Plan of world domination.

When I take over the world, I will give the Elderly One a special place in my kingdom. And I will allow her to eat as many marshmallows as she wants.

I press the Start button. The motor makes a pleasant whirring sound. I am pleased to report that the harness fits me perfectly. It secures around my middle and beneath my rump, thus holding me quite comfortably as I dangle from the drone.

Four blades twirl above my head. I grasp the control box in my paws. There are switches for Takeoff and Landing. There are buttons to move me Up, Down, Right, Left, Back, and Front. What's this button for?

Ahhhhhh!

Apparently that was the Spin button. I shall not press it again.

The dizziness passes. I adjust my crown. I test the controls, moving up and down, left and right. The controls obey me. It is no surprise that I am an excellent pilot—more evidence that I was born for world domination!

The Elderly One and the other humans have gathered in the center of the room. They are waiting for me to give my speech and to lead the parade. To pass the time, a dog is entertaining them with tricks. They shall have to wait a few minutes longer. There is

something important that I must do.

The rat eyes me, jealous that he does not own a flying machine. But that is because he is not an Evil Genius. He gnaws on his cage. I maneuver my Drone of Destiny forward. Whilst carefully balancing the control box in one paw, I open the rat's cage with my other paw.

King Gizmo has set you free! I tell him. *Go forth and spread plague!* He slinks out and disappears over the edge of the table.

Next I open the gerbil cage. They scramble out, thanking me with flicks of their whiskers.

Go forth and chew things! I command. They scurry beneath the tablecloth.

Now to release the most important creatures—the cavies! I open cage after cage.
Come out of your cages! I tell them. A pair
of short-haired cavies step out. A Himala-
yan follows. Three more long-haired cavies
inhale the air of freedom. A gray cavy, a
black-and-white cavy, and an orange cavy
join the others on the table.

*Your days as pets are over. You are now
members of my Cavy Horde!* I tell them. They
look at me with awe and respect. I am giddy
with glee. My Evil Plan is working. My Evil
Horde is forming!

To celebrate, I decide to set everyone free.
I make my way down the length of the table,
opening all the cages.

PRINCIPAL: Watch out, the animals are
loose!
BOY: Spot, why are you swimming in
the punch bowl?

GIRL: How'd my snake get up on the basketball hoop?

ANOTHER

GIRL: Don't step on my hedgehog!

I press the Up button so that I can get a better view. Animals are running everywhere. Humans are chasing after them. Such glorious chaos!

Muh-ha-ha!

That is when barking erupts. Of course, Thorgi is the source of the noise. He and the Toof look up at me. How small they look from way up here, almost as if I'd already put them into the Shrinking Machine. They will try to stop me from giving my speech and leading my parade. They will try to stop me from taking over the world. But they will fail. I am invincible!

I swoop across the gymnasium. Humans scream and duck as I fly over their heads. I hover in the center of the room. Everyone is looking up at me. Finally I have the crowd's attention. This is my chance. I hold up my arms and begin my speech.

Humans, listen up! My name is Gizmo the Evil Genius, and I am your worst nightmare! Soon, all the cavies of the world will be set free and the Cavy Uprising will begin. There is nothing you can do to stop us. You humans will feel my wrath, but for now I hope you enjoy the parade, which is being held in my honor. All hail to me, your future king.

Some of the humans are taking photos, which will be published in history books. I strike a regal pose. But as I do, my Drone of Destiny sputters. It rolls to one side, then to the other side. That dizzy feeling comes back. The machine rolls again. Then it spins. I grasp the control box. I press the buttons, but they do not obey. Spinning. Rolling. My little tummy is not made for such violent movement. I feel queasy. I feel faint. Just when I think I might lose my lunch, the blades stop twirling.

Uh-oh.

For a moment I hang in midair, motionless. My life flashes before my eyes. My carefree days as a pup. My evenings reading to Gweneviere in the pet shop as she waddled on her wheel. My glorious naps in my Eco Habitat. Will this be the end?

An odd sensation takes hold of me, and I realize that I am . . .

. . . falling!

CHAPTER 24

Wedgie

PEOPLE ARE SCREAMING. DOGS ARE BARK-ing. Birds are squawking. There's too much noise in here! Why's there so much noise?

Oh, there's a mouse. I wanna chase that mouse. And there's a snake. I really wanna chase that snake. There are critters every-where. I wanna chase them all. I don't know what to do. What should I do? I'm so excited I start shaking. Hey, why is Furry Potato up in the sky? I wanna chase Furry Potato!

ELLIOT: Don't worry, Gizmo. I'll catch you!

EMILY: Oh no, Pinkie is heading for the door! If she gets outside she might get hurt!

JASMINE: Wedgie, stop Pinkie!

Hey, the door's open. A bunch of critters are running toward it. And there goes Funny Dog. She still has my cape. *Hey, Funny Dog, I bark. Don't go outside. There's a street out there!* If Funny Dog goes outside, she'll be called Bad Funny Dog. And if all those critters go outside, they'll also be Bad. I gotta stop them. I gotta protect them.

I pull on my leash. Jasmine lets go. Then I do what I do best.

MOM: Jasmine, you promised you wouldn't let Wedgie off the leash. He's running wild.

JASMINE: No, he's not. Look, he's herding.

CHAPTER 25

Gizmo

WHERE AM I?

I rub my eyes. My vision clears, and I find that I am lying in a pile of popcorn. I sit up and stuff one of the kernels into my mouth as I try to remember how I got here.

I was piloting my Drone of Destiny and posing for photographers when something happened. But what was it? My thoughts are blurry. My Evil Brain needs fuel, so I eat another kernel.

Elliot reaches down and scoops me into his hand.

ELLIOT: Gizmo, are you okay? You scared me when you fell. What were you doing up there?

I fell?

I peer over Elliot's fingers. The Drone of Destiny lies mangled on the floor. I curl my paws into fists of fury. The machine failed me. It is not worthy of an Evil Genius. *Gadgets and Gizmos* was clearly trying to save money by having gerbils build their drones. Gerbils are dolts! I am enraged! I shall write a letter of complaint and post a bad review!

Elliot tries to soothe me. He holds me in his hands and kisses my head. He hands me my crown, which has been dented by the near-fatal accident. Elliot, my loyal servant, understands my heart-wrenching disappointment.

Thorgi barks. He stands at Elliot's feet, panting and wagging his behind. He

looks . . . proud. Wait a moment. Did the canine tamper with my Drone of Destiny? Is he the reason it crashed? He smiles up at me. Of course! Just like Luke Skywalker destroying the Death Star! Once again, I have underestimated Thorgi's cunning. I shake my fist at him and squeak, *You may have won tonight, but I swear by every Evil Cell in my furry body that one day I will have my revenge on you, Thorgi!*

PRINCIPAL: Attention, everyone. Now that we have caught all the pets, and everything is back in order, let's have our parade!

Some of the humans begin to clap. Others cheer. The human children grab their pets. They begin to form a line.

Is this what I think it is?

Elliot holds me up for all to see. Music starts, and we begin to march. I shiver with excitement. Then I make sure that my crown is firmly set upon my head. My parade begins.

Never fear, dear reader. Thorgi and the Toof may still be regular-size archenemies and my Drone of Destiny may be destroyed, but today ends on a glorious note.

Bow down before your future king!

CHAPTER 26

Wedgie

WE'RE LEAVING NOW. WHAT A GREAT NIGHT. I ate popcorn. I chased three cats. I got to play with Funny Dog. I LOVE this place. I hope we come back.

EMILY: I'm really glad Wedgie was here. He saved Pinkie. She almost got outside.

JASMINE: He's really good at herding.

EMILY: Here's Wedgie's cape. I'm sorry Pinkie took it.

JASMINE: That's okay. I'm sorry Wedgie growled at her.

EMILY: I'm also sorry I copied you.

JASMINE: That's okay. I'm sorry I cared so much about winning.

EMILY: We don't need trophies to know that we have the best pets ever.

I piddle on the fire hydrant. Then I sniff along the sidewalk. Funny Dog follows me. We find a piece of chewing gum. We find a stick. We find something stinky. I don't know what it is, but it's the stinkiest thing ever. I roll all over it. I roll and roll and roll. I LOVE being the stinkiest.

ELLIOT: I thought the pet parade was going to be really boring, but it was a blast!

JASMINE: Yeah, it was funny when that parrot landed on the principal's head.

ELLIOT: You okay that you didn't win anything?

JASMINE: I'm fine. Even though Wedgie didn't win, he was the hero. I love him so much.

ELLIOT: Yeah, me too.

JASMINE: Abuela sure looks happy.

ELLIOT: She sure does!

Jasmine ties my cape around my neck and hugs me. I'm Super Wedgie again! Emily puts the funny hat on Funny Dog's head. Funny Dog shakes her head. The funny hat falls off.

EMILY: I'm starting to think Pinkie doesn't want to be a princess.

JASMINE: I think you're right. I've got an idea....

Come on, Funny Dog. Let's run in circles. I LOVE running in circles. And I LOVE my pack. I run around Mom. I run around Dad. I run around Jasmine and Jackson and Elliot and Emily and Abuela and Furry Potato. Funny Dog runs around Mom and Dad and Jasmine and Jackson and Elliot and Emily and Abuela and Furry Potato. My cape's

flying. And Funny Dog's cape's flying. We both LOVE our capes!

My name's Super Wedgie, and day or night, night or day, I protect my pack, come what may!

DON'T MISS WEDGIE & GIZMO'S
NEXT ADVENTURE!

Wedgie and Gizmo's family is going camping! Wedgie can't wait to herd the tiny squirrels and poop in the woods. But Gizmo has no time for fun. He needs to get all the forest critters to join his Evil Horde. Then they will take over the world, one campsite at a time. Muh-ha-ha!

Bestselling author **SUZANNE SELFORS** lives on a mysterious island in the Pacific Northwest, where she spends most of her time making up stories, which is her very favorite thing to do. She has a dog and a cat, and is seriously considering getting an Evil Genius guinea pig.

You can visit her at www.suzanneselfors.com.

BARBARA FISINGER is an illustrator, character designer, and visual development artist.

You can visit her on Tumblr at www.barbarafisinger.tumblr.com.

When a bouncy, barky dog and an evil genius guinea pig move into the same house, the laughs are nonstop!